# HOW ABOUT A HUG

## By

## Nan Holcomb

## Illustrated By
## Tricia Taggart

ASON AND NORDIC PUBLISHERS

EXTON, PENNSYLVANIA

Books in this series
HOW ABOUT A HUG
ANDY FINDS A TURTLE
DANNY AND THE MERRY-GO-ROUND

HOW ABOUT A HUG

**Library of Congress Cataloguing in Publication Data**

Holcomb, Nan, 1928 -
    How about a hug.

    Summary: Though it takes much concentration and will for her to accomplish each task, a little girl with Down's syndrome is happy to have many loving helpers along the way.

    [1. Down's syndrome — Fiction. 2. Mentally handicapped — Fiction] I. Taggart, Tricia, ill. II. Title.
PZ7.H6972Ho   1987          [E]          87-29734

**ISBN 0-944727-01-8**
Printed in the United States of America

For Jason's friend, Mel

Also for Katie who was a wonderful model
and Michael who pretended he was Andy.

"Good morning, sleepy head," Mommy says.

I say, "Hi!" and sit up in bed.
"How about a hug?" Mommy says.
Do I say yes?

I do say yes.
"I love you," Mommy says and hugs me tight.

"Come, hold my hand," Daddy says. "We'll walk downstairs."
We walk downstairs.
"That's very good," Daddy says. "How about a hug?"
Do I say yes?

I do say yes.
"I love you," Daddy says and hugs me tight.

I eat my breakfast. I get just a little bit of oatmeal
on my chin.
"That's very good," my Grandma says. "How
about a hug?"
Do I say yes?

I do say yes.
"I love you," Grandma says and hugs me tight.

"Let's put on your coat," my brother says.
I hold my arms just so.
"That's a help," my brother says. "How about a
hug for that good job?"
Do I say yes?

I do say yes.
"You're OK, kid," my brother says and
hugs me tight.

Mommy opens the car door and helps me climb in. She fastens the strap on my seat. We're on our way to school.

At school we hold the door and help Andy in.
Andy's my friend.

"How about a hug?" I ask.
Does he say yes?

He does say yes. So, I hug him.

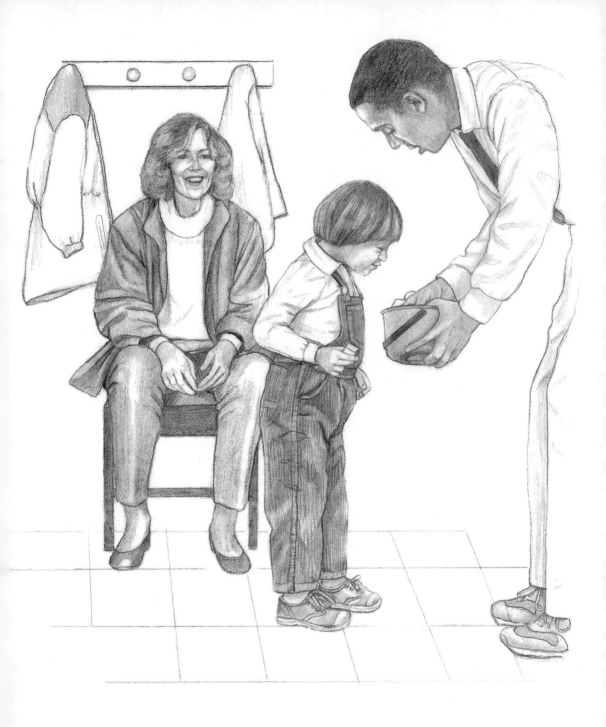

I hug Mommy and say, "Bye-bye!"
Then we're ready to start with our work.

My teacher says, "Let's walk the balance beam."
I try very hard while he holds my hands.

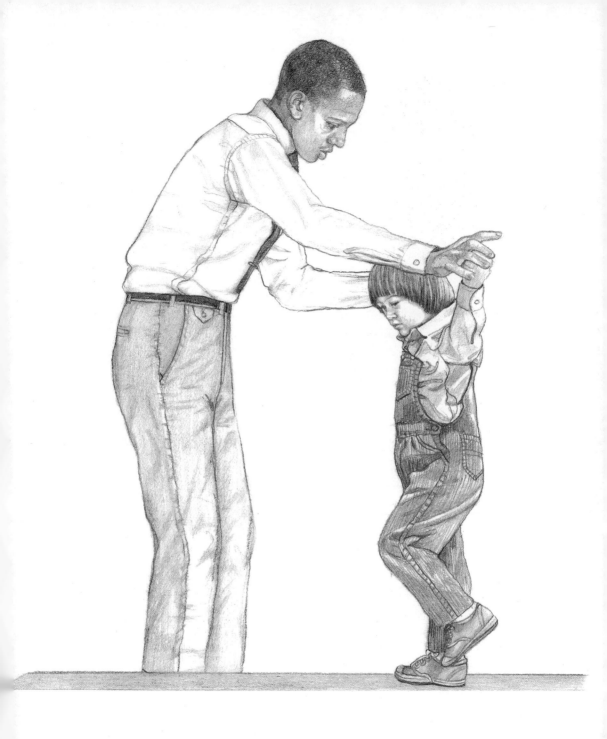

"That's great," he says. "How about a hug?"
Do I say yes?

I do say yes.
"You make me happy when you try so hard,"
teacher says and hugs me tight.

I hold my head up and balance just right on
the big red ball.
My school grandma says, "Great! May I give
you a hug?"
Do I say yes?

I do say yes.
"I love you," School Grandma says
and hugs me tight.

Then I button big buttons on a vest,
put on my shoes,

and take a rest.

Mommy comes back and I say, "Hi!"
"How about a hug?" Mommy says.
Do I say yes?

I do say yes.
She puts on my coat and hugs me tight.

I tell all my friends, "Bye-bye!"

"Come hold my hand," Daddy says. "We'll walk upstairs." We walk upstairs.

I play in the tub.

Put on my nightie
and find my clown.

"How about a hug?"
Do you say yes?

Then I'll hug you tight.
"I love you! Good night!"